Ahoy, mateys! Do you want to join my pirate crew? Then just say the pirate password: "Yo-ho-ho!" As part of my crew, you'll need to learn the Never Land pirate pledge.

TODAY'S PIRATE PLEDGE

A good pirate doesn't take his matey's treasure.

ABDOBOOKS.COM

Reinforced library bound edition published in 2019 by Spotlight, a division of ABDO, PO Box 398166, Minneapolis, Minnesota 55439. Spotlight produces high-quality reinforced library bound editions for schools and libraries. Published by agreement with Disney Press, an imprint of Disney Book Group.

Printed in the United States of America, North Mankato, Minnesota.
092018   012019

DISNEY PRESS
New York • Los Angeles

THIS BOOK CONTAINS
RECYCLED MATERIALS

Library of Congress Control Number: 2017960983

Publisher's Cataloging-in-Publication Data

Names: LaRose, Melinda, author. | Dubuc, Nicole, author. | Character Building Studio; Disney Storybook Art Team, illustrators.
Title: Jake and the Never Land Pirates: Surfin' turf / by Melinda LaRose and Nicole Dubuc; illustrated by Character Building Studio and Disney Storybook Art Team.
Description: Minneapolis, MN : Spotlight, 2019 | Series: World of reading level 1
Summary: Captain Hook has stolen Jake's surfboard! Jake and the crew rush to retrieve it before the board goes over Rainbow Falls.
Identifiers: ISBN 9781532141898 (lib. bdg.)
Subjects: LCSH: Jake and the Never Land Pirates (Television program)--Juvenile fiction. | Surfing--Juvenile fiction. | Theft--Juvenile fiction. | Friendship--Juvenile fiction. | Readers (Primary)--Juvenile fiction.
Classification: DDC [E]--dc23

ABDO
Spotlight
A Division of ABDO
abdobooks.com

Surfin' Turf

WRITTEN BY MELINDA LA ROSE
BASED ON THE EPISODE WRITTEN BY NICOLE DUBUC
ILLUSTRATED BY CHARACTER BUILDING STUDIO
AND THE DISNEY STORYBOOK ART TEAM

Disney PRESS
New York • Los Angeles

Marina the mermaid is teaching
Jake and his crew how to surf.

"Yoo-hoo!" calls a new mermaid. "What a fun surfy-thing. Can I try?"

Who does the mermaid look like?

"That's not a mermaid," says Izzy.

"It's Hook!"

"Look alive, mateys!" yells Skully.

"I see the fin of a sea monster!"

"It's not a monster," says Izzy.
"It's Smee!"
"Now I've got the surfy-thing,"
says Hook. "Let's go!"

How many flowers do you see on the surfboard?

"Those footprints are from Smee's fins," says Jake. "It looks like Hook is heading for Red River," says Cubby.

Can you find Red River on the map?

"Careful, Cap'n," says Smee.
"Don't wake the Tick Tock Croc."

Hook bumps the Croc
with the surfboard.
The Croc begins to chase them!
Hook and Smee jump into the river.

10

"Hook is getting away," says Marina. "They're heading for Rainbow River," says Cubby.

Can you find the Tick Tock Croc?

"Hook is way ahead of us!" says Skully.
"Too bad you aren't mermaids.
Then you could swim down the river,"
says Marina.

"We'll use this wood to help us swim,"
says Jake.
"Yay-hey, that's the way!" says Izzy.

"The river looks like a rainbow flowing down the waterfall," says Smee.

"Did you say . . . waterfall?"
asks Hook.
Hook and Smee cannot stop.
"Lose the surfy-thing!" yells Hook.

Can you name all the colors in Rainbow River?

Hook and Smee jump off the surfboard.
They grab on to a vine.

"Are you okay?" asks Jake.

"We are fine. Move along," says Hook.

"Oh, no! The surfboard is heading toward the waterfall," says Izzy.

"Crackers," says Skully.
"We'll never see the surfboard again!"
"Yes, we will," says Jake.

"I'll lend a helping fin,"
says Marina.
They race toward the surfboard.
"Full speed ahead!" says Jake.

"Be careful, Jake," says Marina.
Jake jumps onto the surfboard.

It is too late!

"Wipeout!" yells Marina.

"We're going over the waterfall!"

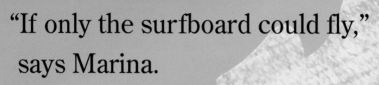

"If only the surfboard could fly,"
says Marina.
"It can!" says Jake.

Izzy sprinkles the surfboard
with Pixie Dust.
"Wheee!" calls Marina.

What does Izzy use
to make the
surfboard fly?

The flying surfboard soars over
Rainbow River.
"Need a ride?" asks Jake.
"Oh yes, thank you," says Smee.

"I don't take rides from puny
pirates or flying fish!" says Hook.
"Whatever you say, Captain,"
says Izzy.

25

"Surf's up!" calls Cubby.
"Let's hit the waves,"
says Izzy.

Jake and his crew have an awesome time!

What do you see on the crew's surfboards?

"We can't hang around all day,"
says Smee.

THUMP! Hook jumps onto a log.
"I'm surfing, Smee!"

Just then, they hear . . .
Tick-tock! Tick-tock!
"That's not a log," says Smee.
"It's the Croc!"

How many logs are in the river?

"What are you waiting for?"
calls Hook.

"Save me, Smee!"

"Right away. Here I come, Cap'n!"
says Smee.

"For solving pirate problems today,
we earned ten Gold Doubloons!"
says Jake.
"Well done, crew," says Izzy.